Curse of the
Crummy Mummy!

JUNIOR MONSTER SCOUTS

#6 Curse of the Crummy Mummy!

By Joe McGee
Illustrated by Ethan Long

ALADDIN
NEW YORK   LONDON   TORONTO   SYDNEY   NEW DELHI

ALADDIN

An imprint of Simon & Schuster Children's Publishing Division
1230 Avenue of the Americas, New York, New York 10020
First Aladdin paperback edition October 2022
Text copyright © 2022 by Joseph McGee
Illustrations copyright © 2022 by Ethan Long
Also available in an Aladdin hardcover edition.
All rights reserved, including the right of reproduction in whole or in part in any form.
ALADDIN and related logo are registered trademarks of Simon & Schuster, Inc.
For information about special discounts for bulk purchases, please contact
Simon & Schuster Special Sales at 1-866-506-1949 or business@simonandschuster.com.
The Simon & Schuster Speakers Bureau can bring authors to your live event.
For more information or to book an event contact the Simon & Schuster Speakers Bureau
at 1-866-248-3049 or visit our website at www.simonspeakers.com.
Series designed by Karin Paprocki
Cover designed by Alicia Mikles
Interior designed by Mike Rosamilia
The illustrations for this book were rendered digitally.
The text of this book was set in Centaur MT.
Manufactured in the United States of America 0922 OFF
2 4 6 8 10 9 7 5 3 1
Library of Congress Control Number 2022936514
ISBN 9781534487468 (hc)
ISBN 9781534487451 (pbk)
ISBN 9781534487475 (ebook)

FOR THE COWS,

who make cheese possible,
and the goats, I suppose, for
your goat cheese contributions

★ ★ ★ ★

· THE SCOUTS ·

VAMPYRA may be a vampire, but that doesn't mean she wants your blood. Gross! In fact, she doesn't even like ketchup! She loves gymnastics, especially cartwheels, and one of her favorite things is hanging upside down . . . even when she's *not* a bat. She loves garlic in her food and sleeps in past noon, preferring the nighttime over the day. She lives in Castle Dracula with her mom, dad (Dracula), and aunts, who are always after her to brush her fangs and clean her cape.

WOLFY and his family live high in the mountains above Castle Dracula, where they can get the best view of the moon. He likes to hike and play in the creek and gaze at the stars. He especially likes to fetch sticks with his dad, Wolf Man, and go on family pack runs, even if he has to put up with all of his little brothers and sisters. They're always howling when he tries to talk! Mom says he has his father's fur. Boy, is he proud of that!

 FRANKY STEIN has always been bigger than the other monsters. But it's not just his body that's big. It's his brain and his heart as well. He has plenty of hugs and smiles to go around. His dad, Frankenstein, is the scout-master, and one of Franky's favorite things is his well-worn Junior Monster Scout handbook. One day Franky is going to be a scoutmaster, like his dad. But for now . . . he wants a puppy. Dad says he'll make Franky one soon. Mom says Franky has to keep his workshop clean for a week first.

GLOOMY
WOODS

LAKE

BARON VON
GRUMP'S HOUSE

CHEESE STORAGE
PYRAMID

CASTLE

GRAVEYARD

CROOKED TRAIL

STARGAZER'S
POINT

VILLAGE

WATERFALL

CHAPTER

1

"IT CAME!" VAMPYRA SQUEALED. SHE was very excited. She was so excited that she ran in circles. Three circles to be exact. That is something you should keep in mind for the next time you are so happy that you cannot contain yourself—run in a circle, three times. Not four. That's too much, and you'll probably just get dizzy.

Franky waved down at Vampyra from the window of Doctor Frankenstein. He

was helping his grandfather with a new experiment.

"Is that what I think it is?" Franky called down.

"All the way from the desert sands, half-way around the world!" Vampyra said. She waved the postcard back and forth. "Hold on, I'll be right up."

Vampyra closed the mailbox. Then she wiggled her toes, snapped her fingers, and closed her eyes. POOF! Vampyra turned into a bat. She flew straight up and through the laboratory window of Castle Dracula.

"Ta-da!" she said, handing Franky the postcard.

"Wow!" said Franky. "This is the coolest!"

"Looks hot to me," said Doctor Frankenstein, peeking over their shoulders. The postcard showed a great big pyramid in the middle of a desert. "All that sand? And sun? Do you know how warm I'd be in my lab coat if I lived there?"

"No, Grandpa," said Franky. "'Cool' means that it's something really awesome. It's, um . . . It's neat. You know, like something really great."

"If you say so," Doctor Frankenstein said with a shrug.

"We have to show Wolfy," said Vampyra.

"Can I go out and play, Grandpa?" Franky asked.

Doctor Frankenstein lifted his goggles from his face. "Would I be a 'cool' grandfather if I said yes?"

"The coolest!" Franky said.

Doctor Frankenstein winked at Franky and Vampyra. "Go on, then," he said. "I can take care of the rest of this contraption."

Franky wasn't sure what Grandpa was building, but it had a lot of springs and bolts and bubbling tubes and coils.

"Thanks, Grandpa!" said Franky.

He and Vampyra raced all the way down the spiral steps and through the main hall and out the front gate of Castle Dracula.

5

"Wolfy, look!" said Vampyra.

Wolfy had just been on his way to visit his friends.

"Is that from Neveen?" he asked.

"Just arrived," said Franky. "She's going to be here in two weeks!"

Wolfy howled in delight, and then he and Franky and Vampyra put their paws and claws together and danced in a circle.

Three circles. Not four. That just would have made them dizzy.

Why were they so happy? What the heck was going on?

The Junior Monster Scouts were about to have an exchange scout come stay with them for the summer. They would get to have a Monster Scout from another place visit Castle Dracula while they learned about each other's customs and culture. It was very exciting, and the first time they'd ever had the chance to do it. Neveen was their soon-to-be-guest's name, and she was from a great big pyramid in an even bigger desert that was halfway around the world!

Isn't that cool?

2

FRANKY AND VAMPYRA WERE NOT THE only ones who heard Wolfy's howl. All the way down the crooked trail, over the river, and clear across the village, two sets of ears perked up at the sound.

Two sets of ears (that's four ears total, in case you were wondering) attached to two heads, atop two rather miserable bodies.

If you had not guessed yet, these ears belonged to Baron Von Grump and his visiting cousin, Baroness Von Grumpier. They lived in the windmill on the edge of the village. A rather empty windmill since Baroness Von Grumpier had recently thrown away all of Baron Von Grump's things. But that's a whole other story—our previous story, to be exact.

But there they sat, in an empty windmill, glaring at each other. Wolfy's howl interrupted their glaring.

"That blasted wolf and his loud howling!" muttered Baron Von Grump. "How am I supposed to sit here and glare with all that noise?"

Edgar, his friend and pet crow, bobbed his head and fluffed his wings. Wolfy's howl had woken him from his nap.

"Finally!" squealed Baroness Von Grump-ier. "Some noise! I simply cannot stand to glare in silence. It's about time there was *some* commotion around here."

Wilma, her friend and pet toad, flicked out her tongue and snatched a fly from the wall. Wilma didn't care one way or the other about Wolfy's howl. She was just hungry for flies.

Baroness Von Grumpier threw open the shutters and gazed out at the village.

"If only there were more noise," she said. "Things are entirely too quiet. If there's one thing I cannot stand, it's silence."

Baron Von Grump's eyebrows drew very close together. So close together that they might have been mistaken for one eyebrow. His face grew red. His mustache twitched. He wished his cousin would just stop talking. He did not want noise. It was the thing he liked least of all!

"Maybe you should . . . go home?" Baron Von Grump said. He tried to smile. It looked like he'd eaten his least favorite food, something he thought was too gross and too yucky to ever swallow. Do you have a food you really don't like at all? Maybe something like mashed lima-bean-and-earthworm pudding? Pretend you have just swallowed a big spoonful of mashed lima-bean-and-earthworm pudding. . . . Now smile at someone. That's what Baron Von Grump's smile looked like.

"I can't," she said.

"Why not?"

"Because all my bags are missing," she said. "No suitcase, no satchel, no bags or boxes."

Baron Von Grump's fake smile slipped away. They weren't missing. He knew exactly where they were. The same place all his furniture and belongings were: at the bottom of the living trash heap on

Stargazer's Point. How did he know this? Because he was the one who had thrown her boxes, bags, suitcase, and satchel away!

As you can see, they were not very nice to each other. They were the opposite of nice.

"Why do you need bags if you have no stuff?" Baron Von Grump asked.

"I suppose I don't," said Baroness Von Grumpier.

Baron Von Grump grinned.

"Because I'm staying a bit longer than planned, cousin," she said.

Baron Von Grump's grin disappeared.

Baroness Von Grumpier clapped her hands together. "This village has so much potential! Why, when I'm done with this place, it'll be the noisiest, busiest, most hectic village you've ever seen! There will be factories and high-rise buildings and lots and lots of roads and bridges and traffic. Come, Wilma, we have work to do!"

Before Baron Von Grump could say anything, Baroness Von Grumpier swept out the door with Wilma.

She slammed the door as loud as she could for good measure.

Then opened it and slammed it again.

3

THE JUNIOR MONSTER SCOUTS COULD hardly contain themselves over the next couple of weeks. They were so excited that Neveen was coming to stay with them that every day felt like a hundred days. Franky had drawn a big red circle on the day she was due to arrive, and every morning they put an X on the current day's spot. Every day they got closer and closer to Neveen arriving. The only thing keeping them from going completely bonkers was watching the construction of the new factory being built in the village.

A new factory?

In the village?

That is exactly what it was, and where it was. After Baroness Von Grumpier left the windmill and slammed the door (twice), she went directly to the mayor. First she complimented the mayor's magnificent mustache. The easiest way to get the mayor to agree to anything was to compliment him on his mustache. He was very fond of it. Then Baroness Von Grumpier told him that she wanted to build a new factory. A cheese factory. And that she wanted to build it right there in the village.

"But why here?" the mayor asked.

"Because *here* is where you make *cheese*,"

Baroness Von Grumpier had said.

"We could make a *lot* of cheese," said the mayor.

"Wheels of cheese as far as the eye can see," said Baroness Von Grumpier.

"It'll be noisy," the mayor said. "Factories make noise, you know. All those machines clanking and whirling and slamming and spinning."

"I know," said Baroness Von Grumpier, smiling.

"It'll be busy," he said.

"Oh, I know," Baroness Von Grumpier said, smiling even more.

"And it will definitely bring more people to the village."

"I'm counting on it," said Baroness Von

Grumpier, smiling so wide that the corners of her mouth touched her ears.

And just like that, the very next day there were bulldozers and dump trucks and construction workers in hard hats hammering and sawing. It was busy, it was noisy, and it was driving Baron Von Grump bananas!

But we're not going to pay too much attention to Baron Von Grump right now. I think we're both more interested in what the Junior Monster Scouts were doing.

They were watching the days of the calendar pass by, anxiously waiting for Neveen to arrive. And when they weren't doing that, they watched the ongoing construction in the village. There were lots of workers and lots of machines, and the new building was going up fast. It was going to be a big factory with three giant chimneys and lots and lots of room for making cheese. Trucks would come from far and wide to pick up the wedges and wheels and drive them off to faraway places. Honking trucks. Rumbling trucks. Trucks with backup beeps and smoggy smoke belching out of them.

One day while the Junior Monster Scouts watched a crane hoist one of the chimneys into place, Vampyra noticed someone waving her hands in the air and jabbing her finger at the map the mayor held.

"Who is that lady standing by the mayor?" Vampyra asked.

"She looks very familiar," said Wolfy.

"She kind of looks like Baron Von Grump," said Franky.

"Oh yeah," said Boris, the leader of the village's rats and the head of garbage removal, "that's Baroness Von Grumpier. The baron's cousin. She's the one building the cheese factory." He rubbed his belly and licked his lips. Boris loved cheese. "To celebrate the village's soon-to-be new factory, she's hosting a Villager Appreciation Day tomorrow. She's going to give out all kinds of free cheese!"

But free cheese or no free cheese, the Junior Monster Scouts had other plans: tomorrow was the day that Neveen was finally going to arrive!

CHAPTER 4

THE NEXT MORNING, THE JUNIOR MONSTER Scouts were up bright and early. The sun had just risen over the mountains when Wolfy, Vampyra, and Franky met out front of Castle Dracula. Even the Little Junior Monster Scouts were there, dressed in their new uniforms. Remember them? The Little Junior Monster Scouts were Wolfy's little brothers and his little sister, Fern. They were training to be Junior Monster Scouts one day.

Franky's windup dog, Sprocket, ran in circles around them, chasing her own coiled spring tail.

"Do you think she's close?" Fern asked. "Is the desert far? When is she going to get here?"

Since Fern asked questions, the rest of the Little Junior Monster Scouts started asking questions as well.

"What's her favorite shape? I hope she likes polygons!"

"Will she hop on one foot with us?"

"Do you think she likes cheese? Do you think she likes *stinky* cheese?"

"Has she ever been to a Snurgle Ball match?"

There were lots of questions, more

questions than I can list here. Wolfy was about to answer as many as he could (he was a very nice big brother), but Vampyra said, "Look! I think I see her!"

Sure enough, something was flying toward them, straight for Castle Dracula. It was Neveen, and she was riding on the back of a sphinx!

A what?

A sphinx.

What's a sphinx?

I'm glad you asked!

A sphinx is a creature with the body of a lion, a cat's head, an eagle's wings, and a snake for a tail. There are different kinds of sphinxes, but this was the kind Neveen had as a pet. Her name was Cleo.

But Cleo sounds *dangerous*, you might be
thinking. A lion's body? A snake for a tail?
Don't worry, Cleo wasn't dangerous. In fact,
the second Neveen landed, Cleo gave Fern

a great big hello lick with her great big cat tongue.

"I think she likes you," Neveen said, climbing down from Cleo's back.

"Welcome to Castle Dracula!" Vampyra said. She gave Neveen a big hug—wrapped her arms right around Neveen's bandages.

Bandages? Was Neveen hurt? No! (But that was very nice of you to ask). Neveen was a mummy, and mummies are wrapped in bandages.

But Neveen was not just a mummy— she was a mummy princess! She lived in a great big pyramid, in a great big desert, with lots and lots of sand and sun and a river so wide and so long, it was like one giant water snake. And speaking of snakes, there were lots of those! Neveen had several pet snakes, but her dad, the king, told her she couldn't bring them. That was probably a good idea. Bringing snakes to your friend's house is usually not something your friend's parents will like.

Don't believe me? Give it a try. Go ask one of your parents if you can have a friend over. Then ask them if they can bring their pet snakes. Snakes, more than one. Like a whole basket of snakes. See what I mean?

"We've been counting down the days until you got here!" Franky said.

"Me too!" said Neveen.

"We can't wait to show you around!" Wolfy said.

"Oh, I brought you something," said Neveen. She handed each of the Junior Monster Scouts a golden beetle pin. "They're called scarabs, and they're a good-luck charm."

The Junior Monster Scouts were so excited. A good-luck scarab! I wish I had a

good-luck scarab. Don't you wish you had one? You could put it right in your pocket and WHAM—instant good luck!

"Thank you so much, Neveen!" Vampyra said. "Come on, let's put your stuff in the castle, and then we'll show you all the cool things around here."

Before they could lift so much as one basket of Neveen's belongings, a very loud banging came from the village. It was followed by an even louder sawing. Then came the rumbling trucks and the growling bulldozers and the smoke-belching diggers. There were workers in hard hats pointing at things and holding up building plans and carrying planks of wood. Another day of construction had begun!

"What in the blazing sands is *that*?" Neveen asked.

"They're building a new cheese factory in town," Franky said.

All the banging and pounding and rumbling and grumbling startled Cleo, and she leaped up into the air and flapped her great big eagle wings.

"Cleo, stay!" Neveen called. "Come back down here, Cleo."

But Cleo didn't listen. She flew higher into the air. She soared in a circle. *They're building something!* she thought. Sphinxes love when things are being built. One of their favorite things is construction. Pyramids, tombs, temples . . . even cheese factories!

Cleo turned toward the village.

"Cleo, no!" called Neveen.

But Cleo had made up her mind. She was going to go see what was being built. Maybe she could even help, she thought!

Neveen groaned and twisted her bandages. "I'm so sorry! Cleo is just a kitten. She is still learning to listen."

"We'd better hurry after her," said Vampyra.

CHAPTER
5

BARON VON GRUMP HAD NOT SLEPT IN days. He thought that maybe with Baroness Von Grumpier spending most of her time in the village (doing whatever it is she was doing—he hadn't bothered to ask), he might finally have some peace and quiet, but no. All the beeping, and hammering, and digging, and sawing had kept him tossing and turning at night and pacing back and forth during the day.

He'd paced so much, he'd worn holes in his socks! He had tried plugging his ears with cotton. He tried wearing earmuffs. He tried covering his ears with pillows. But none of these things worked. Even Edgar had had enough. He'd left the windmill to sleep in the Gloomy Woods. It was much quieter there.

And so Baron Von Grump did one of his least favorite things. He marched straight to the village, earmuffs, pillows, and all. He was going to find whoever was responsible and demand that they stop. And as much as he hated noise, he was going to make himself heard LOUD and clear!

He passed the waving villagers without waving back. He ignored their "Good

morning"s and their "How do you do this day?"s. He did not return their smiles, and he paid no mind to their kite flying, or gum chewing, or Snurgle Ball matches. He strode right into the middle of the construction, took a deep breath, and hollered as loud as he could:

"Who is responsible for all this noise?"

"Why, hello, dear cousin," said Baroness Von Grumpier. "Isn't it wonderful?"

"You?" asked Baron Von Grump. "You're behind all of . . . *this*?"

"I am," she said. "You're looking at the village's brand-new cheese factory!"

Baron Von Grump's eyes widened. His toes curled. His nostrils flared. A factory meant workers, and trucks, and packages, and parcels. Workers and trucks and packages and parcels from morning to night, day in and day out. He might never sleep again. He might never hear his beloved violin. Why, he might never even hear himself think again!

Baron Von Grump turned a light shade

of red, kind of like a pale tomato. Then a little more red, like a rose. And finally, toes curled and nostrils flaring, he turned as red as a fire truck.

But before he could say anything, Cleo landed beside him.

She was very interested in the construction, but there was one thing Cleo loved even more than construction: riddles. Sphinxes *love* riddles. They love riddles so much, and here she was, right next to people she had never met and who had never heard her riddles. She was so excited to ask her riddles that she just blurted one out to the first person she saw (it was hard to miss him—he was as red as a fire truck)—Baron Von Grump.

"What has a head and a tail but no body?" she asked.

Baron Von Grump jumped back four feet (and seven inches, to be exact). He had no idea who this creature was, or where she had come from, or even what she was

talking about. And he certainly had no answer for her question.

"I don't know and I don't care!" he shouted.

But if Baron Von Grump had known he was speaking with a sphinx, he might have tried a little harder to know, and he definitely would have cared. You see, the thing about a sphinx's riddle is that if you don't answer correctly, the sphinx won't say "try again," or tell you you're getting warmer, or stick its tongue out at you and make silly faces. Oh no, that would be too easy! Where's the sport in that? No, the sphinx will turn you to stone!

But wait, you might be thinking. *You said that sphinxes weren't dangerous! You said they were harmless.* Well, yes, I did, but . . . sphinxes can't really control this. They don't want to turn anyone to stone, but that's what happens when you can't answer their riddle. And they can't stop themselves from asking riddles. It's very tricky business.

I don't know and I don't care was not the answer to the riddle.

"Incorrect," said Cleo.

Baron Von Grump's curled toes were the first things to turn to stone. Then his legs, then his body, and finally all the way up to (and right past) his flaring nostrils. Baron Von Grump had been turned to stone!

Now, as cranky and rude as he can be at times, I'm sure we can all agree that Baron Von Grump did not deserve to be turned to stone. Let's hope that the Junior Monster Scouts can do something about this!

But what about the answer to the riddle? Do you know it? Can you guess what it is? If Cleo had asked you, would you have guessed correctly, or would you be turned to stone?

Go ahead and answer. And if you'd like to check to see if you're right, you'll find the correct answer to this riddle, and all the other riddles, somewhere in this book. Where? I can't tell you; that would be too easy. I'll give you a puzzle to figure it out: I'm not up in the front, or stuck in the middle; I'm in last place, so there is your riddle!

Cleo turned to the mayor and asked,

"What has legs but cannot walk?"

"A walrus," said the mayor. "No, a tree. No, a unicycle!"

"Nope," said Cleo.

The mayor was turned to stone.

"A pearl white chest without key or lid, inside which a golden treasure is hid," Cleo said to Baroness Von Grumpier. "What am I?"

Baroness Von Grumpier had no idea. She wasn't any good at riddles. Riddles required thinking, and too much thinking made her brain hurt. She said the first thing that came to her mind.

"Cheese?"

"Wrong answer," said Cleo.

Baroness Von Grumpier was turned to stone, hard hat and all.

"Someone say 'cheese'?" asked Boris.

"The more you take, the more you leave behind," said Cleo. "What am I?"

Boris shrugged. "I give up. What?"

"'What' is not the answer," Cleo said.

Boris was turned to stone.

Cleo flew from construction worker to construction worker asking her riddles. No one could answer. By the time she was finished, there wasn't one hammer swinging, or one tractor chugging.

Everyone had been turned to stone!

You may be thinking, *Those poor people! How can they breathe if they are stone?* And you would be right. But since they were stone, they didn't need to breathe, and so they were okay. It was like taking a nap, only they could not move at all. You can try it right now! Find a fun position to be in and then freeze in place. Don't even move a finger. If someone asks you a question, remain frozen. Your mouth is turned to stone, remember? You cannot move it at all. You can't even look at the person. Go ahead and try it—it'll drive the other person wild . . . unless it's your mom or dad and they tell you to stop being turned to stone and answer them. Then you should probably listen.

"SHE'S PROBABLY HEADED FOR THE NEW factory," said Neveen. "She loves things being built."

But when Franky, Wolfy, Vampyra, Neveen, Fern, and the Little Junior Monster Scouts all reached the village, they were too late. Cleo was nowhere to be found, and everywhere they turned, there was a villager, or a construction worker, or even a trash-carrying rat standing as still as stone.

Well, that makes sense . . . because they *were* stone. Stone statues.

There was a woman flying a kite. A man carrying a basket of radishes. An old woman knitting in her rocking chair. Three kids in the middle of a unicycle race. All the people doing all the things were now stone.

Even the mayor. Even Baron Von Grump. Even Baroness Von Grumpier.

"They're . . . They're *stone*," Franky said. He knocked very lightly on Baron Von Grump's shoulder.

Neveen twisted the ends of her bandages. "Cleo must have asked them a riddle."

"And that turned them to stone?" Wolfy asked. He looked left, right, up, and down

for Cleo. He did not want to be asked a riddle and turned to stone.

"No," said Neveen. "You only turn to stone if you get the answer wrong."

"Yikes!" said Fern.

"Well, what do we do?" Vampyra asked. "How do we turn them back?"

"I never should have let Cleo off her leash," said Neveen. "This is all my fault."

Fern tapped on Baroness Von Grumpier's foot.

"Do you think they are going to *stay* stone?" she asked.

"Not if we can find Cleo and get her to reverse the effects," Neveen said.

"Wait, she can do that?" Vampyra asked.

"She can," said Neveen. "But only because she turned them to stone in the first place."

"She could be anywhere!" Wolfy howled. "She could be halfway back to the desert by now."

Just then Edgar swooped down from the sky and settled on Baron Von Grump's stone shoulder.

"Caw?" he asked. He lightly pecked Baron Von Grump's shoulder. Then a little harder. Then even harder. When he realized he was tapping pure stone, he gave it a few more serious pecks before giving up altogether.

"Caw," he sighed.

"Edgar, have you seen a sphinx?" Franky asked.

"Caw?"

"A sphinx," said Vampyra. "She has the body of a lion."

"And the head of a cat," said Wolfy.

"And eagle wings," Franky added.

"Don't forget the snake for a tail," said Fern.

"And she likes to ask a lot of riffles," said Spike, the youngest cub in the Little Junior Monster Scouts troop.

"You mean riddles," said Neveen. "Her name is Cleo."

Edgar bobbed his head up and down and pointed his wing toward the Gloomy Woods. He'd just tucked his beak under his feathers for a nice nap when she'd landed in his tree, asking him riddles. Edgar, however, had not answered. And by not answering, he was not turned to stone. He simply flew up, up, and away, hoping to find another nice spot to roost and rest.

And then he saw Baron Von Grump standing here, in the village of all places!

But now he knew why. He had been turned to stone.

"Looks like Cleo went into the Gloomy Woods," said Vampyra.

"I know what that means," Wolfy said.

Franky nodded. "Gloomy or not, we have to go in and find her."

The Gloomy Woods were very, very dark. It was so dark that you could hardly see anything, not even your own hand. And there were so many trees. Trees and branches just waiting for you to run into them, or roots waiting to tangle and trip you. The Junior Monster Scouts had gone into the woods once before, when they helped Peter the piper find his kitten, Shadow. They knew how dark and dangerous it was, and they were not thrilled about going in there again.

Neveen clapped her bandage-wrapped hands together. "It won't be so gloomy with this," she said. She held up a glowing yellow stone. "It's a sunstone. It will light our way."

"I don't know," said Fern. "It sounds awfully scary."

Wolfy smiled at his sister and said, "Don't worry, I'll be right there with you."

Wolfy was a very good big brother.

"And remember," he said, "by fur or fang, by bolt or wing, Junior Monster Scouts—"

"And *Little* Junior Monster Scouts," added Vampyra.

"Can face anything!" everyone said at the same time.

"Hands in!" Franky said.

Everyone put their hands together, even Neveen.

"Now let's go find Cleo," Franky said.

Together they left the village and headed up the trail, across the covered bridge, and into the very dark, very gloomy woods.

CHAPTER
7

NEVEEN'S SUNSTONE DID MAKE THE
Gloomy Woods not so gloomy. At least not
the area right around the Junior Monster
Scouts. As long as they stayed close to
Neveen, they had no problem not tripping
over roots, or not bumping their heads on
branches. The scary scampering sounds
were nothing more than bushy-tailed
squirrels. The glowing eyes were just
long-legged deer watching them pass.

The fresh pine and purple lilac created a beautiful aroma. With a little light, the Gloomy Woods really weren't so gloomy after all.

"Cleo?" called Neveen. "Cleopatra!"

They hollered her name. They howled. They made chicken noises. I'm not sure why they made chicken noises, but they did.

But no matter how much they called, or how loudly they called, Cleo did not answer.

"Maybe she's not here anymore," Vampyra said.

"Yeah, maybe she went looking somewhere else to ask riddles," said Franky.

Wolfy groaned. "She could be anywhere! The mayor, the villagers, even Baron Von Grump . . . They might be statues forever!"

Fern tugged Wolfy's sleeve.

"Look," she said, pointing at a nearby tree. "That looks just like your lucky beetle."

"Scarab," Wolfy corrected. "Neveen said it's called a 'scarab.' But you're right, that *does* look just like it. Hey, everyone, check out what Fern found!"

One of the trees had an image of a scarab carved into the bark.

"Nice job, Fern!" said Vampyra. "We would have walked right past that."

Franky took a closer look at the tree. It looked like something sharp had carved the scarab into the tree. Something with claws. Something that just might be a sphinx.

Franky scratched his bolts. He did this when he was thinking. A small blue bolt of electricity crackled between his finger and the bolt on the side of his neck. That happened when he was thinking really, *really* hard.

Franky unpinned his lucky scarab and placed it against the shape on the tree. It matched perfectly! As soon as he held the scarab against the matching shape on the tree, a bright golden line formed around it. There was a flash, and then a loud *POP!* Suddenly there was a stone tablet floating through the air. It was covered in strange symbols and pictures instead of the letters and words that the Junior Monster Scouts knew.

"Magic!" said Vampyra.

"No, hieroglyphics!" said Neveen. "That's how we write things back home. It's an ancient language. Cleo must have written this!"

"Well, what's it say?" asked Wolfy. He tried to read it, but it was very confusing.

"It says . . ." Neveen traced the pictures

with her finger and read aloud. "What always runs but never walks, often murmurs but never talks, has a bed but never sleeps, has a mouth but never eats?"

"That sounds like a riddle," said Vampyra.

"Okay, Junior and Little Junior Monster Scouts," said Franky, "let's put our thinking caps on."

"Do you have an extra?" Neveen asked.

"An extra what?" asked Franky.

"Thinking cap," said Neveen.

"That's just a figure of speech," said Vampyra. "It just means that we need to think extra hard."

"Well, that's for sure," Neveen said. "Because if I know Cleo, her riddles are not going to be easy!"

"This visit is *not* going as planned," said Wolfy.

It certainly was not. And are you thinking what I'm thinking, dear reader? Are you thinking that Neveen is right, that Cleo's riddle is not easy at all? This riddle sure seems like a hard one!

"Maybe we should think about this one part at a time," said Franky.

"That's a good way to approach a riddle!" said Neveen.

"Hmmm," said Vampyra. "What runs but never walks?"

"A car!" said Wolfy.

"A refrigerator!" said Fern.

"My nose!" said Spike.

None of those seemed like they would

lead to the right answer. No one could figure out how a refrigerator, a car, or Spike's nose murmured, or had a mouth but never talked.

"This is a really hard riddle," said Franky. "And the longer it takes us, the more of a chance that those statues will stay statues forever."

"Or that we'll get turned to stone too!" said Wolfy.

At that very moment, when they were thinking they'd never come up with the answer, Franky's lucky scarab began to glow. A small cloud formed in front of him, and it began to rain.

"Franky, look," said Neveen. "Your scarab is giving you a clue."

"A clue?" Franky asked. "It looks to me like all I'm getting is wet boots." Franky's eyes widened. "That's it!"

"What's it?" asked Vampyra.

"Yeah, I don't get it," said Wolfy. "Water?"

"Water runs, right?" Franky asked. "Well, what kind of water has a mouth, and a bed, and murmurs as it moves along?"

"Not a lake," said Wolfy.

"Not the bathtub," said Fern.

"Not the waterfall," said Neveen. "We flew over that when we first arrived at Castle Dracula."

The waterfall couldn't be it, thought Vampyra. But then she remembered what came *before* the waterfall.

"A river!" said Vampyra. "That's the

answer! Cleo wants us to go to the river!"

"A river has a mouth, and a bed at the bottom, and murmurs and babbles as it runs," Franky explained.

"Great job, Junior Monster Scouts!" said Neveen. "We'd better hurry."

They followed Neveen and her sunstone out of the Gloomy Woods and hurried for the river.

CHAPTER
8

"THERE'S THE MOUTH OF THE RIVER," said Franky, pointing to where the lake emptied into the wide ribbon of water that ran all the way to the edge of the cliffs.

"I don't see Cleo," said Neveen.

"Maybe our friend Laguna saw her," said Vampyra. "She lives in the lake and swims in this river all the time."

Wolfy proudly pointed to his Swimming

Merit Badge. "Mrs. Lagoon taught us all how to swim."

Fern tugged her brother's scout sash.

"Wolfy?"

"Yes, Fern?" he asked.

"I don't think Laguna is going to be able to tell us where Cleo went," Fern said.

Fern was right. Neither Laguna nor Mrs. Lagoon were going to be able to tell the Junior Monster Scouts anything. They were sitting beside the river, very still and very much turned to stone. Not only were they turned to stone, but so were five fish all lying along the riverbank, and several ducks.

"We're too late," said Neveen. "And at this rate, there won't be anyone *not* turned to stone besides us."

The Junior Monster Scouts were beginning to feel very deflated. They had no one to tell them where Cleo went, and they had to stop her before every person, monster, fish, duck, frog, and rat was turned to stone!

Wolfy picked his way along the riverbank.

"Aha! Look what I just found!" said Wolfy, holding up a large, round, smooth river stone. "Cleo left us another clue."

The stone had a picture of a beetle on it, just like the tree in the Gloomy Woods had. Wolfy did what Franky had done. He placed his own lucky scarab on the picture, and just like the tree in the Gloomy Woods, the stone began to glow. There was another bright flash and another loud POP, and then a floating stone tablet appeared.

Neveen read the hieroglyphics.

"Everyone has me, but nobody wants me—yet I'm still collected and regularly emptied. What am I?"

"That's another tough one," said Vampyra.

"It's too tough," said Fern.

"But what does everyone have?" said Wolfy. "Fur?"

"I don't have fur," said Neveen. "I have bandages. What about skin? Hair? Claws?"

"What about a shadow?" asked Vampyra, looking at Wolfy's shadow on the water. "Everyone has a shadow!"

"They do," said Franky, "but people don't want to get rid of their shadow."

"I love my shadow," said Spike. "You can make funny animals with it. Look, here's a giraffe!" Spike made a shadow puppet of a long-necked giraffe.

"And what is collected and then emptied?" Wolfy asked.

Wolfy's lucky scarab began to glow, just like Franky's had.

A crinkled tin can appeared in the grass, rolling along the riverbank.

"Look at that," said Vampyra. "Litter!" She picked up the can. "I'll make sure this gets thrown away."

Wolfy jumped in the air and howled.

"It's a clue," he said. "And I think you just figured it out, Vampyra."

"I did?" she asked.

"What is collected but regularly emptied?" asked Wolfy.

Vampyra held the crinkled can up. "Ohhhhh . . . garbage!"

"Everyone has it, but nobody wants it," said Franky. "Except for maybe Boris and the rats, but I'd say they're an exception."

"Could Cleo be at Stargazer's Point?" asked little Fern.

"Only one way to find out," said Wolfy. "Everyone, follow me!"

Wolfy led the Junior Monster Scouts, Little Junior Monster Scouts, and Neveen away from the river's mouth and out to

Stargazer's Point. That was where the village's trash was dumped, and that was where they hoped they'd find Cleo and help her realize that this wasn't just a game, that the villagers couldn't stay stone forever.

CHAPTER
9

STARGAZER'S POINT WAS A VERY STINKY place. The villagers put all their garbage in bins and boxes, and then Boris and the rats brought that garbage here, piling it into one big, towering heap of rubbish: moldy banana peels, dirty socks, tin cans, and fish bones. Rusted springs, coffee grounds, fuzzy cheese, and sour milk.

Do you want to know how bad it smelled? Take a pair of your shoes that you wore

all day, maybe ones that you wore without socks. Now put your nose in your shoe.
Take a big, deep breath! Gross! You just
smelled your stinky shoe! But at least now
you might have an idea of how smelly the
garbage heap was.

The flies loved it. The rats treasured

it. And the Trash Heap ate it. She was very good at keeping it all contained on Stargazer's Point, and now she had babies to feed. That's right! The Trash Heap had made a home on Stargazer's Point, and the villagers had given her so much trash since then that she had little trash babies . . . several little Trash Heap babies that were always hungry for more smelly trash!

But when Wolfy and his friends arrived, Madame Trash Heap did not shuffle forward to say hello. The babies did not open their mouths wide and cry for more gross garbage. The rats didn't put on a show-and-tell of the things they found in the villagers' tossed-out trash.

Because as you have probably guessed,

Madame Trash Heap, and the babies, and the rats were all turned to stone.

"We're running out of places to check," said Franky. "We've been to the village, to the Gloomy Woods, to the lake and river, and now here."

"Look," said Neveen, "what's on that old boot?"

"It's another beetle," said Vampyra. "Cleo must have left us another riddle."

"I'm not sure how many riddles I can handle," said Wolfy. "My brain hurts!"

"Go ahead, Vampyra," Franky said. "Use your lucky scarab."

Vampyra placed her gold beetle against the image on the boot, and just like the tree, and the stone, there was a glow and a *POP!*

Another stone tablet with hieroglyphics appeared.

"Tall and old and made of stone," Neveen read, "the opposite of day might call me home. What am I?"

Do *you* know what the answer is? Can you figure it out? I'll give you a minute to think about it. . . .

"The opposite of day is night," said Franky. "What does night call home?"

"The sky?" Vampyra asked.

"Yeah," said Wolfy. "That's where the moon lives."

"We howl at the moon all the time," said Spike. He began to howl, and the rest of the Little Junior Monster Scouts howled with him.

"But that doesn't have anything to do with stone," said Neveen. "What's tall, and old, and made of stone?"

Franky scratched his bolts again. You know what that means—he was puzzling things out. Franky was a very good puzzler.

"What if it's not 'night,'" he said, "but 'knight,' with a *k*?"

"And everyone knows where knights live," said Wolfy.

"In a castle!" said Vampyra. "Cleo has gone to the castle!"

"You didn't even need a clue for that one," said Neveen. "You're becoming pretty good at solving riddles."

"We have to," said Franky. "We can't let everyone stay statues forever."

"I know," said Neveen.

"And if we don't solve them and find Cleo soon," said Wolfy, "everyone at Castle Dracula might get turned to stone next."

"Good point," said Vampyra. "Follow me!"

She spun in a circle one time . . . two times . . . three times, and *POOF!* Vampyra turned into a bat.

She flapped and flittered off toward Castle Dracula, and everyone quickly followed.

CASTLE DRACULA WAS VERY BIG. IT HAD lots of rooms and lots of stairs and lots of towers for Cleo to hide in. But when the Junior Monster Scouts ran across the drawbridge and into the front hall, they found her curled up in front of the fireplace. It was a big fireplace, but Cleo was even bigger. Imagine finding a creature the size of a car curled up in front of your fireplace.

"All that flying around and asking riddles must have tired her out," said Neveen.

"I hope she's not too tired to turn everyone back to normal," said Franky.

Neveen sat down next to her pet sphinx and gently stroked her soft fur. Cleo yawned in her sleep and stretched her long legs and large paws. Her eagle wings unfurled, and her snake tail rattled. She was so comfortable that she began to purr.

She opened one yellow eye, and then the other. When she saw the Junior Monster Scouts and Little Junior Monster Scouts all gathered behind Neveen, she sat up and let out a very loud meow.

"Cleopatra," said Neveen. "Have you been asking people riddles?"

"Meow," said Cleo.

That meant "Yes."

"And did you turn them to stone?" asked Neveen.

"Meow meow," said Cleo.

That meant "Yes, because they did not answer my riddle correctly."

"That is not a nice thing to do, Cleo," said

Neveen. "Especially not when we're guests here."

Cleo meowed and licked her paw.

"Meow meow meow," she said.

"I know that's the rule of riddles," said Neveen, "but we're not in the desert. We're not back home with the pyramids. We're guests here, and we should be on our best behavior."

Cleo twitched her tail and rubbed her paw behind her ear.

Franky raised his hand.

"I have a new game. What if we answer one more riddle, Cleo?" Franky asked. "If we get it right, you turn everyone back. If we get it wrong . . . then you can turn us to stone."

"Franky!" Vampyra said.

"What are you thinking?" Wolfy said.

"I don't wanna be turned to stone!" said Fern. The other Little Junior Monster Scouts agreed.

Franky smiled.

"Any problem can be solved when all your friends get involved," he said. "I think we've gotten pretty good at these riddles, and I'll bet we can solve this one too."

"Okay," said Wolfy.

"If you think so," said Vampyra.

"Ask away, Cleo," said Fern.

Cleo thought for a moment. She was excited to ask the Junior Monster Scouts a riddle, but she wasn't sure which one. She had so many!

Finally, she sat up straight, cleared her throat, and spoke in a language they could all understand. (If all her riddles were in meows, nobody would ever be able to solve them!) This is what Cleo asked: "What do you find at the end of a rainbow?"

The Junior Monster Scouts and Little Junior Monster Scouts gathered in a circle.

"Okay, what's at the end of a rainbow?" Franky asked.

"Grass," said Wolfy. "It ends in the grass."

"But what if it lands in the lake?" Vampyra asked. "Maybe it's water."

"Could be water or grass," said Franky, "so that can't be it. What about gold? Everyone knows that leprechauns hide their pots of gold at the end of the rainbow."

Fern listened while the Junior Monster Scouts puzzled over the answer. She was thinking too. Sometimes it helped her to write down parts of the questions. She used her little claw to scratch RAINBOW on the stone castle floor.

Do you know the answer to the riddle? What do you find at the end of a rainbow? The clue is right in front of you. . . .

RAINBOW.

Franky, Wolfy, and Vampyra stopped puzzling. They looked at what Fern had written, and then, at the same time, the answer came to them. It was right there in front of their faces.

The answer to Cleo's last riddle was—

CHAPTER
11

OH, HELLO THERE.

Are you waiting for the answer?

Did you guess? I didn't want to reveal the answer until you had time to think about it. You think you know what the answer is?

What is your answer?

Are you sure?

Are you really, really sure?

Really, really, *really* sure?

Okay, well, let's see if you're right.

CHAPTER

12

FRANKY, WOLFY, AND VAMPYRA TURNED
to Cleo and said, "W! The letter *w* is what
you find at the end of a rainbow!"

Cleo smiled.

"Meow!" she said.

That meant "correct"!

"Wow," said Neveen. "You didn't even
need a clue, or to use your lucky scarabs.
You're riddle-solving champions!"

"Good enough to have earned your

Riddle Merit Badges," said Dracula, suddenly appearing behind them in a thick cloud of mist.

"But how did you know we solved all those riddles?" asked Wolfy.

Wolfy's dad, Wolf Man, entered the front hall. "A wolf has excellent hearing," he said. "I heard each riddle *and* heard you solve them. They were difficult! Even Doctor Frankenstein had a tough time with some of them, and he's a supersmart scientist!"

Franky's grandfather, Doctor Frankenstein, and Franky's dad, Frankenstein, came down the winding stone steps from the laboratory tower.

"That's true," said Doctor Frankenstein. "They were very clever riddles."

"But you've all earned another patch," said Frankenstein. "Even you, Neveen."

"Even me?" she asked.

"Yes," said Frankenstein. "You each get a Scout Exchange Merit Badge." He handed each of the Junior Monster Scouts and Little Junior Monster Scouts a yellow patch with a pyramid on it. He gave Neveen and Cleo a blue badge with a castle on it.

"That's for sharing your culture with one another," said Wolf Man.

"Speaking of culture," said Dracula, "it's probably about time that Cleo returned everyone to normal."

"Meow," said Cleo.

That meant "I'm sorry" and "You're right."

Cleo got down low on the ground, and Neveen climbed onto her back.

"Everyone, climb on!" she said.

Wolfy, Franky, Vampyra, Fern, and the rest of the Little Junior Monster Scouts clambered onto Cleo's back. Cleo sprang into the air, and with three quick flaps of her wings, they soared out of Castle Dracula.

"The castle looks so small," said Franky.

"Wheeeee!" said Fern.

Neveen pointed to the village, and Cleo flew toward the cheese factory, and all the people she had turned to stone.

"Look, there's the mayor!" said Vampyra.

"And Baron Von Grump," said Wolfy.

"And his cousin Baroness Von Grumpier," said Franky. "She looks grumpy enough to crack stone!"

"Okay, Cleo," said Neveen. "Reverse your magic!"

Cleo swept around the construction site and around the village. Wherever her tail swished, sparkles of golden lights settled on whoever had been turned to stone. One second they were a statue, and the next second they were back to normal.

It was like nothing had happened. Nothing at all. No one even had any idea that they had been turned to stone. They all picked right back up where they had left off—the woman flying a kite, the man carrying the basket of radishes, the old woman knitting in her rocking chair, and even the three kids in the middle of their unicycle race.

The mayor was just putting on his construction hard hat. The rats were hauling off trash. Baroness Von Grumpier was reading blueprints and supervising construction. And Baron Von Grump was red-faced and angry at all the noise, noise, noise, NOISE.

Cleo flapped her wings and went from place to place, turning everyone back to normal. Laguna and Mrs. Lagoon and all the fish and ducks. Madame Trash Heap and her trash babies and the rest of the rats.

And when she was done, she landed right back in the village.

"Meow," she said, purring.

"That means 'I promise to be on my best behavior for the rest of our trip,'" Neveen told the Junior Monster Scouts.

Cleo even gave the mayor one great big apology lick.

"Well, that's good," said Vampyra,

"because we can't keep answering riddles and turning people *back* from stone the whole summer!"

"She also says she has one more thing to do," said Neveen.

"Oh yeah?" asked Wolfy. "What's that?"

CHAPTER
13

DO YOU REMEMBER WHEN I TOLD YOU that sphinxes love building things? Well, Cleo wanted to build something for the villagers. The new cheese factory was what had gotten Cleo's attention in the first place. And since they were so close to being done, and Cleo felt so bad, she used her magic to do the last of the work.

She put the last beams in place, put up the last wall, and even lowered the roof onto the new factory. Baron Von Grump suddenly found himself without a grump to gripe about. There was no more hammering, or sawing, or bulldozing, or banging.

"It's too big," he growled. "It's an eyesore."

"I know," said Baroness Von Grumpier, wringing her hands. "Isn't it atrocious?

There's going to be so much cheese, and so many trucks."

That gave Cleo one last idea. If there was going to be that much cheese, they would need a place to store it all. They would need a cheese warehouse. Better yet, a cheese pyramid!

Cleo swept up, up, up into the air, and quicker than you could say, *Pick a pyramid packed with packaged cheese* (go ahead and try saying that three times in a row), she had built the villagers their very own Cheese Storage Pyramid . . . right next to Baron Von Grump's windmill.

"That's it!" roared Baron Von Grump. "You win! You all win! You can all have your cheese factory, and clanking trucks, and Snurgle Ball, and gum chewing, and 'good morning's and 'How do you do?'s!"

"Oh?" asked Baroness Von Grumpier, raising one bushy black eyebrow. "And what of your precious windmill?"

"You can have it!" said Baron Von Grump. "Good riddance!"

Baron Von Grump stomped off to collect his things (two things, really: his violin and his picture). That's all he had left.

"Caw!" said Edgar, flying after him.

That meant "Wait for me!"

But that wasn't the last the Junior Monster Scouts, or the village, would see of Baron Von Grump. And Baroness Von Grumpier didn't win that easily. But that's a story for another day. Perhaps the next story.

But this story ends with one last riddle, of course. You see, the Junior Monster Scouts had a riddle for Cleo.

"What goes in your pocket, but keeps it empty?" Franky asked.

Know the answer?

Ready to earn your Riddle Merit Badge?

I think you are.

So . . . what's your answer?

Are you sure?

Are you really, *really* sure?

Well, turn the page. Let's see if you're correct.

RIDDLE ANSWERS

R: What goes in your pocket, but keeps it empty?

A: A hole

R: What has a head and a tail but no body?

A: A coin

R: What has legs but cannot walk?

A: A table

R: A pearl white chest without key or lid, inside
which a golden treasure is hid. What am I?

A: An egg

R: The more you take, the more you leave behind.
What am I?

A: Footsteps

JUNIOR MONSTER SCOUT
· HANDBOOK ·

The Junior Monster Scout oath:

I promise to be nice, not scary. To help, not harm. To always try my best to do my best. I am a monster, but I am not mean. I am a Junior Monster Scout!

Junior Monster Scout mottos:

By paw or claw, by tooth or wing, Junior
Monster Scouts can do anything!

Never say "never" when friends work
together!

By tooth or wing, by paw or claw, a Junior
Monster Scout does it all!

When someone else is in trouble, we help
them out on the double!

Any problem can be solved when all your
friends get involved!

Junior Monster Scout laws:

Be Kind—A scout treats others the way
they want to be treated.

Be Friendly—A scout is open to everyone, no matter how different they are.

Be Helpful—A scout goes out of their way to do good deeds for others . . . without expecting a reward.

Be Careful—A scout thinks about what they say or do *before* they do it.

Be a Good Listener—A scout listens to what others have to say.

Be Brave—A scout does what is right, even if they are afraid, and a scout makes the right decisions . . . even if no one else does.

Be Trustworthy—A scout does what they say they will do, even if it is difficult.

Be Loyal—A scout is a good friend and will always be there for you when you need them.

Junior Monster Scout badges in this book:

Riddle Merit Badge

Scout Exchange Merit Badge

· ACKNOWLEDGMENTS ·

Jess, you know all the things I want to say, so I'll just leave it at this: I love you, and I'm beyond grateful that we have each other. And cheese, am I right? Maybe we need a cheese storage pyramid of our own?

To our collective, combined, wonderful blended family: Shane, Logan, Sawyer, Zach, Ainsley, and Braeden, thank you for being you and for being a part of *our* story. You are all inspirations!

Mom and Dad, thank you for keeping my bookshelves stocked, my library card current, and my imagination fed while I grew up. I'm really grateful for that.

To my superstar agent, Jennifer Soloway,

thank you for everything you do, and for being such a champion of my work. I'm a very lucky author to have you in my corner.

Karen Nagel, thank you, thank you, thank you. I continue to grow as a writer under your amazing editorial wizardry. Being able to work with you is a dream come true. And thank you to the entire Aladdin team— from layout to copyediting to the art team and design to marketing and all the people involved and departments I might be leaving out. Thank you all for the attention and work you put into making these books.

And finally, thank you, reader, for opening this book and reading it and (hopefully) loving it just as much as I do.

READ ON FOR A PEEK AT
NIGHT FRIGHTS,
A SPOOKY SERIES FROM JOE McGEE.

A cold wind rattled the windows, but Madeline did not look up. She stared at the chipped, white porcelain of her plate. Not at the plate itself. Not at the smeared remnants of what had been her mashed potatoes. Not at the remaining crumbles and gristle and fat of her pork chop, or the bone pushed aside. No, Madeline stared at the small pile of pale-green lima beans in the center of her plate.

She stared at their wrinkled little skins, at the fine, bristly hairs that poked up here and there, and at their weird kidney shape.

"Madeline Harper," said her mother, "eat your lima beans."

"No."

"No?" her mother repeated. "What do you mean 'no'?"

"I mean," said Madeline, looking up from her plate for the first time in fifteen minutes, "that I am not eating those disgusting lima beans."

"Lima beans are *not* disgusting," her mother said, "and I won't take no for an answer."

"Mind your mother," said Madeline's grandmother, pointing her fork at Madeline.

Madeline glowered. Her grandma was the

one who'd bought the lima beans in the first place.

"They're mushy, they taste like dog throw-up, and they make my tongue itch," said Madeline. She set her fork down and leaned back in her chair, arms crossed. "I'm not eating them."

"They're good for you," said her mother.

"Don't you want to be healthy?" Grandma asked. "You are what you eat, after all."

"Well, I certainly don't want to be a lima bean," Madeline said. "Who'd want to be a wrinkled, gross, green, pathetic excuse for a vegetable that no one likes?"

Madeline's mother stood up and carried her own clean plate over to the sink.

"Well, you can sit there until you eat them," she said.

"But, Mom—"

"I won't hear another word about it," her mother said. "The sooner you clean your plate, the sooner you can get up from the table."

Outside, the fierce gale hammered the shutters again and shook the house.

Madeline sat alone at the table, watching the hands of the clock slowly crawl along. Fifteen minutes, twenty, a half hour. Her mother was watching television. Somewhere in the living room, Grandma was knitting.

Madeline's dog, Tucker, lay curled at her feet under the table. He whined at the storm and looked up at her, nose sniff-sniffing what was left on her plate.

"I wouldn't even feed these beans to you,

Tuck," said Madeline. "And you eat beetles."

Tucker whined again.

"Madeline Harper," said her mother, standing in the kitchen doorway. "Eat. Your. Lima beans."

Madeline dragged her fork across her plate. It made an awful screech.

"I. Said. No."

Madeline's mother pointed down the hall.

"That's it, young lady," she said. "Go to your room. Now!"

Madeline pushed her chair away from the table and stalked to her room. Tucker followed.

"And I am leaving these lima beans right here until you decide to eat them!" her mother called after her.

Madeline slammed her bedroom door.

Madeline tried to read, but she couldn't concentrate. She pushed a few pieces around her chessboard. She dusted her chess trophies and organized her bookshelf. She tried to do a crossword puzzle, but she just couldn't stop being angry about being sent to her room for not eating lima beans.

READ & LEARN
with
simon kids

Keep your child reading, learning,
and having fun with Simon Kids!

A one-stop shop where you can
find downloadable resources, watch interactive author
videos, browse books by reading level, and more!

Visit us at
SimonandSchusterPublishing.com/ReadandLearn/

And follow us @SimonKids

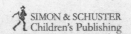

SIMON & SCHUSTER
Children's Publishing

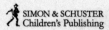